Biscuit
Goes to School

story by ALYSSA SATIN CAPUCILLI
pictures by PAT SCHORIES

Sandy Creek

For the wonderful students, teachers,
librarians, and parents who have
welcomed Biscuit into their schools!

Here comes the school bus!

Woof, woof!

Stay here, Biscuit.

Dogs don't go to school.

Woof!

Where is Biscuit going?

Is Biscuit going to the pond?

Woof!

Is Biscuit going to the park?
Woof!

Biscuit is going to school!

Woof, woof!

Biscuit wants to play ball.

Woof, woof!

Biscuit wants
to hear a story.
Woof, woof!
Shhh!

Biscuit wants a snack.

Woof, woof!

Oh, Biscuit!

What are you doing here?

Dogs don't go to school!

Oh, no!

Here comes the teacher!

Woof!

Biscuit wants
to meet the teacher.
Woof!

Biscuit wants
to meet the class.
Woof, woof!

Biscuit likes school!

Woof, woof!

And everyone at school
likes Biscuit!
Woof!